ATop the Tree Top
A Christmas Story

By C. Brian Taylor
Illustrations By Sharon Butler

Or Visit The Rilly Silly Book, Co. at:
www.rillysilly.com

Library of Congress Catalog Number: 2003098404 **ISBN 0-9747054-0-3**

For Andrew
You're big! You see, you're three!
—Dad

For John
—S.B.

In merriment
Our family spent
Their time around the tree
But quietly they did not see
The ornament who called to me.

"Hello...Hello..." came a whisper from the Christmas tree.
"I'm Bonnie Blue!
And it was you,
If you remember,
Who made me last December
With some paper and some glue?"

"Yes, I guess, more or less, I remember you."

"Well, as the ornament,
    Though slow in my descent,
I guess you could say have been sort of—*sent*
    To have you come and walk with me."

"Who me? But I'm too big to walk inside a tree!"
said I, the little boy,
with his shiny new toy,
"I'm big! You see, I'm three!

"Yes, you're big compared to me," said Bonnie Blue,
"But close your eyes,
Forget your size
And please, oh please, won't you walk inside
This Christmas tree with me?"

"Say...may I bring my little sister?
I think I would miss her, if it's okay with you?"

"Of course, it's fine.
Take her hand
For it's time
To follow
This fading blue swallow
As we wind
'Round
The hollow
Of this pine!

You see,
Year in and year out
Ornaments are put away,
Forgotten
For months
And months
And months
Until that special day
When we are taken out
And placed about
The branches of this tree.

And today, this Christmas day,
You'll get to be an Ornament like me!"

"But what do Ornaments do, Bonnie Blue?
Do they open presents like we children do?"

"No, no, come with me
And soon you'll see!
Follow this swallow and we'll show you what to do."

"Rickety Rick, Rickety Rick!
I walk with a walking stick.
And even though
My wooden bones
Bring moans
        And moans
            And moans,
                Being older makes me bolder!

Halt! I'm Rickety Rick, a rickety-quick toy soldier!"

"Do Ornaments stand guard, Bonnie Blue?"

"Yes
child,
Yes,
they
do.
They keep a careful eye over children like you.
    Rickety Rick may be made of wood,
    But he's an older stick soldier,
    An Ornament who sticks to helping others, wouldn't you?"

"I'm Bouncy Bouncy Bear!
I have a lot of hair!
Except for there and there
And there
And there
And there.

I'm Bouncy Bouncy Bear,
It's Beary nice to meet you!"

"Do Ornaments bounce like Bouncy Bear, Bonnie Blue?"

"Why
Yes!
Yes
Child,
They do.

Bouncing helps others bounce a little too!

Though she's made of cotton balls
And raisins for her ears,
Bouncy Bouncy Bear is an Ornament who cares
By bouncing,
        Bouncing   here   or   there
Bouncing,
Bouncing everywhere!

will get there!
we Ornaments
and together,
to your get up
and others will step up
in your step up
Put a bounce step

Over there is Rocky Horse Sally
And Red Bulb O'Mally
The Green Light Family
And the Popcorn Rally.
Don't dilly-dally, we have a ways to go!

I love the little Bells
 They ring
 And ring
 And ring
They have a precious little sound
They make me want to sing—I'm a singing bird, you know.

And now we've come to Candy Cane Lane
Where crooked staffs
Have spots like leopards,
Lots and lots of spots—except for certain types,

The ones with stripes—the stripes of the shepherd."

"Are Ornaments supposed to herd their sheep, Bonnie Blue?"

"Why
Yes,
Yes
Child
They do.

Especially the weak sheep too.

And now the most important part!
But before we start,
We have cause to pause and
Stop.

We stop
Atop the Tree Top!   Shhhhhh.

For you must be certain
Before we pass this TINSEL CURTAIN
That you're an Ornament through and through!

I'm Bonnie Blue,
And you are who you are.
We've come so very far
May I present to you. . .

. . . The Star!"

I'll always remember . . .
As a child in December
When I walked as an ornament that day,
But the light of that star
Burned so brighter far
Than the shiny toys I got as a boy that day.

And today when I put the Christmas decorations away,
I made a choice to hear a little voice—
It was Bonny Blue who peeked out of the box to say,
    "Tattered or torn
    Rusty or worn
    It doesn't matter to him.
    We've come from afar
    To honor the Star,
Can it be wrong to honor Him all year long... *the* Ornament we adorn?"